STAR WARS™

BB-8 FINDS A FRIEND

WRITTEN BY NATE MILLICI

ART BY PILOT STUDIO

Disney • LUCASFILM

P R E S S

Los Angeles • New York

D0888190

All rights reserved. Published by Disney Lucasfilm Press, an imprint of Buena Vista
Books, Inc. No part of this book may be reproduced or transmitted in any form or
by any means, electronic or mechanical, including photocopying, recording, or by any
information storage and retrieval system, without written permission from the publisher.
For information address Disney • Lucasfilm Press, 1200 Grand Central Avenue,
Glendale, California 91201.

Printed in China

First Boxed Set Edition, October 2016   10 9 8 7

Library of Congress Control Number on file

FAC-025393-22178

ISBN 978-1-4847-9036-6

Visit the official *Star Wars* website at: www.starwars.com.

Meet BB-8.

BB-8 is a little orange droid.

He is one of a kind.

He beeps and boops

and rolls this way and that.

One day, BB-8 was on a
mission with his master.
His master's name was Poe.
BB-8 saw something in the sky.
It was First Order ships.

The First Order
was looking for a map.
The map would help lead
to a lost Jedi Knight.

But a man named Lor had
given Poe the map.
BB-8 warned Lor and Poe
about the First Order.
BB-8 and Poe needed to leave.
Lor needed to hide.

BB-8 and Poe rushed to their X-wing.
But the First Order saw them.
The First Order blasted their ship.
BB-8 and Poe could not fly away.

Poe gave BB-8 the map.

Poe told BB-8 to hide.

Poe promised to come back for BB-8.

BB-8 rolled away over the dunes.

BB-8 was worried about Poe.

But he was also worried
about himself.

BB-8 did not want to be alone.

Meet Rey.
Rey looks for parts
in old crashed ships.

She loads the things she finds
onto her speeder.

She trades them for food.

Then she goes back to her home.

Rey is lonely.

One day, Rey heard
a beeping sound.

It was BB-8!
He was trapped in a net.

Rey cut BB-8 free.
BB-8 was no longer alone.

BB-8 followed Rey home.

At first, Rey told BB-8
to leave her alone.
BB-8 was sad.

Then Rey told BB-8 he could stay
for one night.
BB-8 was happy.

The next day, they went
to the market for food.

The mean alien Rey traded with offered to buy BB-8.

Rey told the mean alien that
BB-8 was not for sale.

Rey was happy to know BB-8.
BB-8 was happy to know Rey.
Rey and BB-8 were happy
to be friends.